THE
Bubble Gum
Monster
STRIKES AGAIN

Marilyn D. Anderson
illustrated by Estella Hickman

Published by Willowisp Press, Inc.
401 E. Wilson Bridge Road, Worthington, Ohio 43085

Printed in the United States of America

10 9 8 7 6 5 4 3 2

ISBN 0-87406-405-8

Contents

Spud Learns A New Trick

That crazy Spud! Spud's my dog. Most of the time he's okay, but sometimes he's really something. Like last Saturday, I was sitting on my bed when a lamp flew past me. Then a wastebasket hit me on the head.

I turned around fast. Spud was standing with his back paws on my pillow and his front paws on my dresser.

Mom stuck her head in the door. "What's going on in here?" she asked.

"Spud broke a lamp," I said. "He was trying to get this piece of bubble gum. It was in the wastebasket. And that's why I

had the wastebasket on top of the dresser."

"Oh, dear," she said. "Remember all the trouble Spud had with bubble gum last spring?"

"I can't believe the fire department had to cut off his fur to get him unstuck from all the bubble gum he chewed!" I answered.

Spud was looking at my piece of bubble gum and drooling.

Mom looked at Spud. "He chews so much gum, I'm surprised he can't blow bubbles," she said with a laugh.

Bubbles, I thought to myself. That's a great idea! But I didn't say anything about it then. Learning to blow bubbles turned out to be very hard for Spud. He watched me blow a whole bunch of bubbles, but that didn't help him learn. Finally, I gave up. "Who ever heard of a dog that could blow

bubbles, anyway?" I asked out loud.

Sunday afternoon, I was up in my room again. Spud was with me. He found a piece of bubble gum and gobbled it right up. For

a while, I heard him pop and snap the gum. But then things got very quiet.

I looked at Spud. He was making strange faces.

"What's the matter, Spud?" I asked. "Is your mouth tired from chewing?"

Spud grinned a big toothy smile. Then a tiny spot of pink appeared at the corner of his mouth. After a second the pink spot seemed to grow a little. Then it disappeared.

I kneeled down next to Spud. "Hey, Spud," I asked. "Was that a bubble?"

He wagged his tail and spit out the gum.

Maybe I'm just seeing things, I thought. I tried to get Spud to take the gum back.

"Here, do it again," I said.

But Spud turned away. You see, he never chews used gum. Spud likes only brand new gum.

I opened a new piece.

"Here," I said, handing Spud the piece of

gum. "Blow another bubble."

Spud gobbled the gum and began to chew. He closed his eyes. I could tell he was enjoying the gum. But I didn't see any bubbles.

"Hmm," I said. "I guess I just imagined the whole thing."

Then Spud opened his eyes and gave me a strange look. His mouth opened a little. This time, I could see a small pink bubble in his mouth. "Spud!" I cried, giving him a big hug. "You did it! You blew a bubble!

10

Wait until Mom sees this."

But before I could move, the bubble popped. And Spud spit his gum out again.

"Mom, come here!" I yelled. Before I knew it, Mom and Dad came running into my room.

"What's the matter, Sam?" Dad asked.

"Spud learned a new trick," I said. "Watch this!"

I handed Spud another piece of gum, and I waited. And I waited. And I waited. Spud chewed and chewed. Mom sniffed.

"What's he supposed to do?" she asked.

"Just watch," I said.

We waited some more.

After a long time, Mom asked again, "What's he supposed to do?"

"He's learned how to blow bubbles," I told her.

"Sam, that's impossible," Dad said. "Dogs can't blow bubbles."

"Shhh," I said. "He has to concentrate."

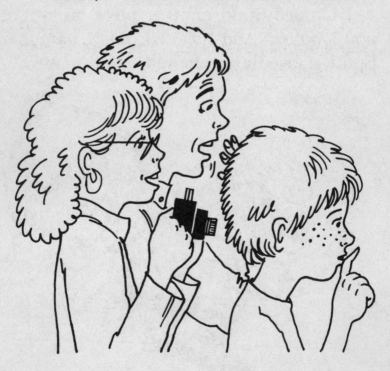

Mom and Dad looked at each other. I could tell they didn't think Spud could blow bubbles. We all waited for what seemed like hours. And then something pink and gooey oozed from Spud's mouth. It grew just a bit before Spud swallowed the gum again.

"Good heavens!" Mom cried. "That did look like a bubble. I'm going to get my camera." And she dashed from the room.

"I think that was just a glob of gum falling out of his mouth," Dad said. "Dogs can't blow bubbles."

"It *was* a bubble," I said. "I'll get some more gum."

I got another piece of gum for Spud. We watched him chew and chew. But nothing happened. He just chewed the gum and stared back at us.

"Well, I don't think anything's going to happen," Mom said. "I guess I'll go make supper." And she left with her camera.

"Sam," Dad began, "I hope this will teach you not to—"

But I wasn't listening to him. "Dad!" I cried, pointing at Spud. "He's doing it again!"

Dad stared at Spud. "Holy cow!" he shouted. "That is a bubble!"

"I told you he could blow bubbles," I said, hugging Spud. "Just wait until the kids at school hear about this."

Dad frowned. "Sam, are you sure you want to tell the kids at school about this?" he asked.

"Why not?" I asked.

"Well," he said, "they may not believe you. They think you made up your adventure with the firemen last spring."

Later that night, I decided not to tell everyone that Spud could blow bubbles. But I just *had* to tell my best friend Freddy.

2
No One Believes Me

I told Freddy the whole story on the way to school the next day.

"That's some trick," he said. "I bet Spud could be on TV with that trick."

"I don't think so," I said. "He's shy."

I figured that was as far as my story would go. But I was wrong. Freddy told everyone in school about Spud.

By the end of the day, everyone had heard that Spud could blow bubbles. Even our teacher, Miss Brings, had heard. She came back to my desk.

"Sam," she said softly. "These tall tales about your dog only get you into trouble with the other children."

"They're not tall tales," I protested loudly. "Spud really can blow bubbles."

"Well, maybe you just thought you saw him blow a bubble," she said.

Jason Brown turned around. "It's all right, Miss Brings," he said. "We know Sam makes up those stories."

"But I'm telling the truth," I said.

"Prove it," said Shannon Smith from across the aisle. "Bring in your dog for show and tell."

"Do it, Sam," Freddy said. "Spud could be a star."

"Yeah, bring your dog to school!" the rest of the class shouted.

Uh-oh. What am I getting Spud and myself into? Spud didn't do anything for Mom's camera. He might not blow bubbles

for the kids at school, either.

"Well, I—I can't," I sputtered. "It's against school rules."

I figured that would quiet everyone. Then Daniel said, "But we're studying animals, Miss Brings. Please let Sam bring in his dog so we can study a real live animal."

Miss Brings thought for a moment.

"Well, maybe we could let a dog come to class just this once," she said.

Oh, no, I thought. Now my goose is really cooked.

Freddy babbled about Spud's bubbles

the whole way home. He wanted my dog to become a star. But all I could do was worry.

I told Mom and Dad everything at the supper table that night. Spud took his usual place right under the table. He wagged his tail every time I said his name. Spud likes to sit under the table because sometimes food drops onto the floor, and then he can gobble it up. We were having meat loaf for supper. I don't like meat loaf too much, but it's Spud's favorite food. He likes it as much as he likes you know what—bubble gum.

"So, now you see why I have to take

Spud to school for show and tell," I finished.

Mom had a worried look on her face. "Oh, Sam," she said. "I really wish you wouldn't. You know what a problem that dog can be."

"But I have to, Mom," I said, squirming in my chair. "The other kids think I'm making up stories about Spud."

Dad looked up. "I was afraid of this," he said. "That's why I asked you not to tell anybody about those bubbles."

"But I only told Freddy," I said. "He blabbed it all over school."

"Well," Mom said finally, "I guess you

can take Spud to school. But you'll have to be careful."

"And don't let Spud eat too much bubble gum," Dad added.

"Oh, thanks," I said, getting up from the table. "Can I go practice with Spud?"

"Okay, Sam," Mom said.

I called Spud out from under the table. At first he didn't want to come out. He was waiting for some meat loaf to fall onto the floor. Then I showed him some gum, and we went running up to my room.

Spud and I practiced for an hour. I was sure Spud could blow bubbles whenever he wanted to. But would he want to blow bubbles? I was worried that the old bubble gum monster could strike again if I took Spud to school. And I was right.

3

Spud Goes To School

The next day, Spud and I got to school early. Miss Brings was the only person around. She gave Spud a rug to sit on. We put the rug next to my desk.

Soon the other kids started to come into the classroom. Everyone was nice to Spud. Some kids even tried to give him bubble gum. But I told them not to. They'd have to wait until show and tell.

Spud seemed to like school. He sniffed everyone and wagged his tail.

Then the tardy bell rang.

RRRRIINNNNGGGG! Spud jumped to his feet. He barked and tried to run out the door. The other kids laughed, and Spud didn't like that. He gets nervous when people laugh at him.

After that, I could barely keep him on his rug. He wouldn't sit still.

Miss Brings said, "Sam, you may bring Spud to the front of the room now."

That's when I started to get nervous. I

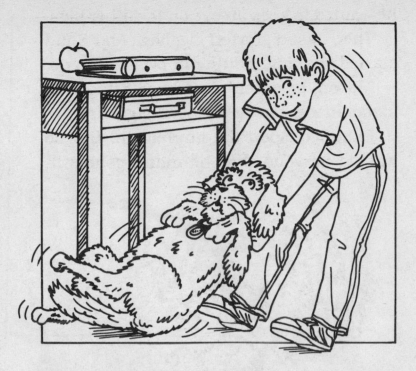

could tell that Spud was nervous, too. My knees started knocking. Maybe Spud's knees were knocking, too. I couldn't tell. It's hard to see a dog's knees.

I got to my feet and tried to smile. "Come on, Spud," I said.

But Spud didn't want to go. I had to drag him to the front of the room. He whimpered. I pulled. When we got to the front of the room, I tried to make Spud face me. But he wanted to keep an eye on the other kids.

Then Jason started giggling. And Spud started shaking. I didn't know what to do.

"Jason, be quiet," said Miss Brings. He made a face, but he stopped giggling.

I showed Spud the gum again. But he was so nervous that he didn't gobble it.

First he sniffed the gum. Then he licked it. Then he picked it up with his lips. He chewed it very slowly. I could feel all the kids watching Spud and me.

Spud started to work the gum around in his mouth. The kids looked at each other

and grinned. Then Spud popped the gum. I was sure he'd blow a bubble any second.

But I don't think the other kids had ever seen a dog pop bubble gum before. They all started to whisper about it. And that made Spud nervous again. He stopped chewing and spit out the gum.

"Shhh!" I demanded. "Spud can't concentrate if you're talking."

"That's right, class. You'll have to be quiet," said Miss Brings. "Now, Sam," she continued. "We'll let you try this one more

time." I saw Jason wink at Shannon. And Freddy looked worried.

"Okay," I agreed. "I know he'll do it this time if everyone will sit still and be really quiet."

Miss Brings sighed. "We'll try," she said.

The room was so quiet that it was almost scary. I gave Spud some new gum, and he chewed slowly. Everyone's eyes were fastened on Spud. He stared back at them. The clock in the room clicked forward. It sounded as loud as an airplane taking off. Spud chewed until we were all stiff from trying to be so still and quiet. Just when I thought it was hopeless, I heard someone shout, "Look at that!"

Something small and pink showed up on Spud's lips. It was a bubble!

"HOORAY!" the kids shouted. They leaped from their seats to clap and whistle and cheer.

"He did it! He really did it!" cried Freddy, knocking his books all over the floor.

Jason looked surprised. "I guess Sam was telling the truth," he said.

Miss Brings took a closer look. "Well, it certainly looks like a bubble," she said. "I can't believe it—a dog who blows bubbles."

I was so proud of Spud that I gave him a great big hug. He wagged his tail faster.

Then there was a rush of kids to the front of the room. Everyone wanted to hug

Spud. I got bumped out of the way. Then I saw what else they were doing. That's when I got really nervous.

"No!" I shouted. "Please don't give him any more bubble gum!"

But no one heard me. They were all
shouting and cheering. Jason gave Spud
four pieces of gum, and Spud gobbled them
right up. Spud's second bubble was four
times as big as the first bubble.

"Yahoo!" the kids screamed. "Give Spud more gum!" And that's what they did. They all threw gum in front of Spud. The pink pile of bubble gum grew and grew.

Spud loved it. He ate piece after piece and blew bigger and bigger bubbles. He was the star of the class, and he knew it. But I was getting really worried. I promised Dad I wouldn't let Spud have too much gum.

And this was definitely TOO MUCH!

4
Stop, Spud! Stop!

"That's enough, class," Miss Brings said. "It's time to get back to work. Sam," she said, "take Spud back to his rug now."

I wanted to take Spud back to his rug, believe me. But Spud wouldn't stop chewing the gum. He had a whole pile of gum in front of him. I knew he wanted to chew it. His next bubble was so big that it almost splattered on Miss Brings.

I tried to get to Spud. But everyone was standing around him. "Don't let him have any more gum!" I shouted.

But it was hopeless. Spud was wild about the gum, and the kids were wild about Spud. He gulped the pink stuff in bigger and bigger batches. And he blew bigger and bigger bubbles. The kids were yelling and screaming with delight. The classroom was a madhouse.

What could I do? I pushed my way through to Spud and dived for his stack of gum. But Spud saw me coming. He gobbled all the rest of the gum in one mighty gulp. Then he looked at me. His tail was wagging a mile a minute.

"You crazy dog," I said. "You're going to

make yourself sick."

But he didn't look sick. He looked like he was having a great time. He started chewing the whole mess. I knew what was coming next.

"Oh, no!" I yelled. "Stand back, everybody! This one is going to be humongous! It's going to be a monster."

Spud's monster bubble grew and grew. It caught up all the books and all the papers on all the desks. It took all the chalk and all the erasers off the blackboard tray.

It got our jackets and hats. It swallowed the
science projects on the back table. Our
class turtle tried to crawl away. But turtles
can't crawl very fast, and the bubble gum
monster got it, too.

Still the bubble gum monster grew. It started picking up desks and tables and chairs. I screamed when I saw what the bubble grabbed next. Freddy, Jason, and Shannon disappeared into the pink goop.

And the monster bubble kept on growing.

"Get down on the floor!" Miss Brings yelled.

But we weren't even safe on the floor. The bubble swallowed Joe, Jon, and Beth. Then it went for Terri and Robert. It got Brent over by the lockers. Jenny and Julie were standing on the science table. But the

bubble gum monster reached up and pulled them down, too. Will was trying to escape out a window. He never made it.

I heard Miss Brings yell, and then she was gone. The monster ate her, too.

I was the last one left. I saw the big pink bubble gum monster heading straight for me. I turned to run, but there was nowhere to go. I felt a tug on my leg. And then I was swallowed up, too!

We couldn't see anything. We were all

stuck inside a huge pink blob. I could hear kids screaming.

"Yaghhh!"

"Aiieee!"

"Helppp!"

I heard another sound, too.

"Arff!"

Spud had been eaten by his own bubble. He was caught in the pink mess with us.

"Help!" we all cried. "Somebody save us from the bubble gum monster!"

"Yeooow!" howled Spud.

Suddenly, we heard the classroom door open. We heard the voice of Mr. Todd, the principal. He started to come in. "All right, what's all the noise...?" he began to say.

But then we heard Mr. Todd scream.

"Arrgghh! My foot is caught in a big pink glob!"

We heard Mr. Todd grunting and groaning. He was trying to pull his foot loose.

Then we heard a groan, a pop, and a shout. Mr. Todd was free.

But from inside the humongous pink bubble, we saw his brown shoe, stuck in the goo. The bubble gum monster had eaten the principal's shoe.

"Good heavens!" shouted Mr. Todd. "I'll go call the fire department!" And we heard the door slam.

The fire department? Uh-oh. Not again!

The Bubble Gum Monster Strikes Again

Soon we heard sirens. We heard voices in the hall. We heard footsteps getting closer to our classroom. Then the door opened.

Mr. Todd said, "There it is, Chief. It's getting bigger. It's a real monster."

"Watch out!" shouted the chief. "Everybody stand back, please!" Then he said, "Go ahead, and pop it, Mike. But be careful. That pink blob has eaten all the kids, and it could eat you, too!"

We heard the sound of chopping and

poking. Suddenly, we saw a sharp metal point poke through the bubble gum monster. There was a tremendous pop and a big explosion. And then we were free from the bubble gum monster.

What we saw was a horrible mess. Everyone and everything in our classroom

49

was covered with sticky pink bubble gum. It covered the lockers. It dripped from the ceiling. There were globs on the desks, globs on the chairs, globs on the chalkboard, and globs on the lights. We couldn't move because we were all stuck in the pink stuff.

The firemen were the same ones that had come to my house last spring. But luckily they didn't see me.

"What's all this pink stuff?" asked a
fireman. "It looks like bubble gum. It
feels like bubble gum. It smells like
bubble gum."

"It is bubble gum!" cried Miss Brings.
"And don't just stand there talking. Get
us out of here!"

"It's bubble gum?" one fireman asked.
And all the firemen started laughing.

One of the firemen said, "It looks like

the bubble gum monster strikes again!"
They all laughed some more.

"What's so funny?" Mr. Todd asked.
"This is a disaster. A bubble gum disaster. And I'm going to find out what
happened."

"Uh-oh," I said.

The chief sent his men to get some
tools. Then the chief said to Mr. Todd,

"The reason we laughed is that we had another bubble gum disaster last spring. Some kid and his dog got gum all over everything."

"Oh, is that so?" said Mr. Todd.

The firemen came back with more tools and a can of oil. The fireman named Mike poured oil on an ax so the bubble gum wouldn't stick to it. He started hacking his way through the gum.

The oil wasn't working. Before long, the ax got caught in the gum. And then Mike's boots got stuck, too. He couldn't

move.

"This isn't working," said the chief. "We need the leaf sucker, Tony."

"Right, Chief," said another fireman. "I'll get it."

Tony came back in a few minutes with a long metal tube that they use to suck up dead leaves from the streets in the fall. The tube was connected to a big machine out in the hall. Tony started to move the metal tube around the classroom. The machine started chugging.

With a loud whoosh, the tube started to suck up the bubble gum—and everything else.

I felt myself slowly moving toward the leaf sucker. The first person to get

to the leaf sucker was Mike, the fireman. Just before the leaf sucker sucked him up, the other firemen chopped Mike out of the gum. He was free.

One by one, everyone was pulled toward the sucker, and the firemen cut everyone loose. As the kids got free, they all helped the firemen pick things out of the gum before the leaf sucker sucked them up. They picked out desks and chairs, pencils and paper, and hats and coats. I saw Freddy pick out the class turtle. They stacked everything in the hall.

Miss Brings got free from the pink

stuff. And then it was my turn. The chief cut away the gum, and took a long look at me. "Hey," he said. "Aren't you the same kid we rescued last spring? Is this mess your fault, too?"

"Not exactly, Chief," I said.

Mr. Todd heard us. He asked the chief, "Has Sam done this before?"

"Not exactly," I said again.

"No," said the chief. "Last time, the gum was all over the street, not a classroom."

"Sam, how do you get into these messes?" Mr. Todd asked.

I shrugged and said, "I don't know,

Mr. Todd. My dog just likes bubble gum, I guess."

"Today was an accident," explained

Miss Brings. "We wanted Spud to blow bubbles for us, and he did. But the kids got carried away."

The firemen were cutting Spud free.

They had to cut off a lot of his fur—
again.

"Ha-ha! Look at that haircut!" Jason
shouted, pointing at Spud.

Spud just whimpered.

Miss Brings said, "I see a lot of gum
in your hair, too, Jason. You might look
funny when you get a haircut." Jason

stopped laughing.

"Excuse me," said a voice. A lady with a notebook was standing next to Mr. Todd. "Are you the principal of this school?" she asked.

Mr. Todd tried to smile. "Yes," he said. "I'm afraid I am."

"I'm from the newspaper," said the lady. "I'd like to do a story on your school. Your students seem to really like school."

Mr. Todd smiled a great big smile. "Why, yes, they do like school," he said. "Step into my office. I'll tell you all about our school."

All right! I thought. Maybe he'll forget about Spud and me.

Finally, the firemen had sucked most of the bubble gum out of our classroom. They took away the leaf sucker. But the room was still a mess. We had to shovel a lot of gum into trash cans and plastic bags.

The janitor brought rags, soap, and water. The whole class helped clean the room. Some of them scrubbed the floor.

Some washed the desks. I cleaned the turtle.

Finally, the place looked as good as new. It took all day to clean everything up. When we finished, it was time to go home. But I couldn't find Spud.

"Here, Spud. Come here, boy." I called and called, but he didn't show up.

I went into the hall and looked around. "Hey," I called out. "Where's Spud?"

We all looked around. Suddenly, I noticed a wagging tail sticking out of the top of a garbage can.

"Spud!" I shouted, running toward the garbage can. "Spud, what are you doing?"

I looked down into the garbage can. What do you think I saw? Spud was

after another piece of bubble gum!

"Spud, you crazy dog!" I yelled as I dived into the garbage can after him. "No more bubble gum for you! Not now! Not ever!"